OPERATION KANGAROO TRAP

by Spencer Strange

with

Andrea Menotti ← words

and

← **Kelly Kennedy**

pictures

Scholastic Inc.

New York Toronto London Auckland Sydney
Mexico City New Delhi Hong Kong Buenos Aires

Visit the Spy Five web site at
www.scholastic.com/spyfive!

Your new password is:

kangatrap

Use this password
to access a new
game!

ISBN 0-439-70350-6

Copyright © 2004 by Scholastic Inc.

Design: Julie Mullarkey Gnoy

12 11 10 9 8 7 6 5 4 3 2 1   4 5 6 7 8 9/0

Printed in the U.S.A.

First printing, November 2004

CHAPTERS

Have fun keeping
your secrets out
of sight!
— Spencer

CHAPTER 1
THE BIRTHDAY SURPRISE

It all started when Anika found out that Miss Pryor's birthday was coming up. We had no idea how old she was going to be, of course—maybe twenty-something, maybe thirty-something, or maybe even forty-something. Somewhere up there.

Anyway, Anika wanted to give Miss Pryor a present.

"I have the perfect thing," Anika said. "My little brother got a Kangarate toy for his birthday last month, but he already *has* two of them. He gave the new one to me, 'cause I thought it was kind of cute. But I don't really want it anymore."

"So you want to *re-gift* it to Miss Pryor?" Ursula asked.

"If you want to put it that way," Anika said.

"Actually, you're *re-re-gifting* it," Ursula said. "'Cause someone gave it to your brother, and your brother gave it to *you*."

"It's still a *gift*," Anika said defensively. "It's not like it's *used* or anything."

Kangarate, the karate kangaroo

"Then why don't you just return it?" Julian asked. "Or exchange it?"

"We don't have the receipt," Anika said. "My aunt sent it all the way from California."

"You could always sell it online, like on e—" Blitz started to suggest, but Anika cut him off.

"Look, if you guys don't think it's a good idea, then think of something else. I just thought it was a really cute gift 'cause of the martial arts connection," Anika said.

"It *is* a good idea," I assured her.

"Yeah, Kangarate is perfect for Miss Pryor," Blitz agreed.

"It can be from all of us," Anika said. "As a 'thank you' for all her help."

"And for being the first person we ever spied on," Ursula said.

"And for giving us kung fu Fridays," Julian said.

And so it was settled.

✷ ✷ ✷ ✷

Miss Pryor's birthday was on Thursday, so we met that morning in the hall outside her room. Anika brought the Kangarate all wrapped up in birthday paper, and Ursula brought a card she'd made on her computer.

"**SURPRISE!**" we all said as we walked into the room. "**HAPPY BIRTHDAY!**"

a wrapped Kangarate!

Miss Pryor looked totally shocked.

"How did you *know?*" she asked.

"We have our ways," Anika said, handing Miss Pryor the gift and the card.

"*Happy Xth birthday,*" Miss Pryor read aloud. "That's the Roman numeral for 'ten,' you know. I'm just a *little* older than that."

"How old *are* you?" Julian asked.

"*Old,*" Miss Pryor said firmly.

"Will you tell us in Roman numerals?" Julian tried.

"Or in dog years?" Blitz suggested.

"Nice try," Miss Pryor said, quickly changing the subject to the gift. "What's this?"

"Open it!" Anika said excitedly.

"You really shouldn't be spending your money on me," Miss Pryor said.

"Oh, don't worry—we didn't..." Ursula started to say, but we all gave her "what-are-you-thinking" looks and she put a cork in it.

Miss Pryor opened the wrapping paper very slowly and carefully, like it was a treasure. *Finally* she pulled the Kangarate out.

"*Oh,*" she said, looking kind of puzzled. "How sweet."

"It's Kangarate," Anika explained.

Miss Pryor still looked puzzled.

"Haven't you heard of Kangarate?" I asked.

"And his sidekick Ninjaroo?" Blitz asked.

"They're on TV in the morning," Anika said. "They're *really* popular."

"Press the buttons on his back," Blitz said. "He punches and kicks."

"And jumps and head-butts," Julian added.

 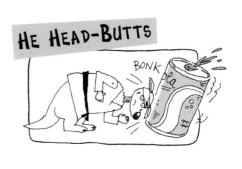

"Well, isn't that fun," Miss Pryor said with a smile.

"We thought you'd like it 'cause it's martial arts," Anika said.

"It's very sweet of you to think of me," Miss Pryor said. "I'll put it right here on my desk."

She placed the Kangarate next to her tea mug.

"Have a great birthday," Anika said.

And we all said similar birthday-wishy things and headed out.

✳ ✳ ✳ ✳

Later that day, Ursula came up to me and Julian in the hall.

"I know a way we could find out how old Miss Pryor is," she said.

"How?" I asked.

"We could ask her questions like, 'What was your favorite movie when you were a kid?' And then we could look up when that movie came out," she said.

"But what if she liked old movies?" I asked. "And didn't she grow up in China? Wouldn't the movies have been different there?"

"Good point," Ursula said. "I'll think of some other questions during silent reading."

Julian and I said we would, too.

✳ ✳ ✳ ✳

When silent reading was finally over, Julian and I met in the hallway and compared questions.

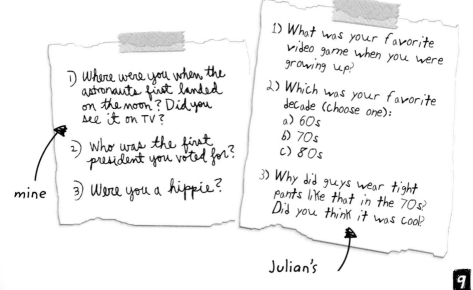

mine

1) Where were you when the astronauts first landed on the moon? Did you see it on TV?

2) Who was the first president you voted for?

3) Were you a hippie?

1) What was your favorite video game when you were growing up?

2) Which was your favorite decade (choose one):
   a) 60s
   b) 70s
   c) 80s

3) Why did guys wear tight pants like that in the 70s? Did you think it was cool?

Julian's

Ursula arrived a little later, and we showed her the questions we'd come up with.

"I like the moon question," Ursula said. "And the video game one is pretty good, *if* Miss Pryor *played* video games."

"Well, at least we can get her talking," I said. "And see what other clues she drops."

"True," Ursula said. "And then we can ask her my clincher question."

Ursula's clincher question

What's your Chinese zodiac sign?

"Why would we ask *that?*" Julian asked.

"*Because*," Ursula said. "Your questions will get us in the right *decade*, and then *my* question will zero in on the exact *year*."

"Chinese zodiac is by year?" I asked. "Not by month?"

"Exactly," Ursula said. "There are twelve Chinese zodiac signs, and they repeat every twelve years. So if we know *about* when she was born, we can figure out the *exact* year by finding out her sign and checking a zodiac calendar."

"Cool," I said. "Let's go talk to her after school."

* * * *

So, after a few rehearsals, Julian, Ursula, and I went to visit Miss Pryor after school. She was sitting at her desk grading papers when we walked in.

"Hello, you three," she said cheerfully. "What brings you here?"

"Oh, we just came by to chat," Ursula said. "If you have a second."

"Sure," Miss Pryor said. "What did you want to chat about?"

"We were just curious what life was like when you were a kid," I began, just liked we'd planned.

"Like did you play video games?" Julian asked.

"Oh, no," Miss Pryor said. "My father was very strict. We pretty much just read books and put together jigsaw puzzles."

"You couldn't even watch TV?" I asked.

"Only on very special occasions," she said.

"Like when *Apollo 11* landed on the moon?" I asked.

"That was before my time," Miss Pryor said with a smile. "But yes, events like that we were allowed to see."

"Like which events?" Ursula asked.

"Oh, the Olympics," Miss Pryor began. "Things like that. Sometimes we were allowed to see movies. Of course, kung fu movies were my favorites. And I remember once seeing a fabulous nature special on termites that was just fascin—"

"Miss Pryor," Ursula suddenly interrupted. "Where's Kangarate?"

And all of our eyes immediately went to the spot on the desk where she'd put Kangarate that morning.

It wasn't there.

Where's Kangarate?

Miss Pryor's face looked like this

"Did you move it?" Ursula asked.

"No...it was right here..." Miss Pryor said, rummaging around her desk.

"When did you last see it?" Julian asked.

"I put it beside my mug in the morning when you were here, and then..." Miss Pryor trailed off.

"Was it here during our math class?" Ursula asked me and Julian. "I didn't look over here."

"Me neither," I said, and Julian said the same thing.

"I'm afraid someone must have taken it," Miss Pryor said, shaking her head in disbelief. "I just can't believe someone would *do* such a thing."

"*Believe it,*" Ursula said flatly. "This school is a den of thieves."

"I'm so sorry I wasn't more careful with your gift," Miss Pryor said. "I feel terrible."

"It's not *your* fault," I assured her.

"And it's not definitely gone forever," Julian said. "We can try to track it down."

"Yeah," Ursula said. "We'll conduct an investigation."

"I appreciate the thought," Miss Pryor said. "But I think it's best if I handle it myself."

"But what are you going to *do*?" Ursula asked.

"I think I'll just make a *gentle announcement* at the beginning of all of my classes tomorrow," Miss Pryor said. "It might turn up."

"I raise my doubt card," Ursula said bluntly.

"Your *what*?" Julian asked.

"My *doubt card*," Ursula said. "It means I highly doubt that the pathetic thug who stole Miss Pryor's Kangarate will suddenly develop a conscience."

"You're such a pessimist, Ursula," Miss Pryor said.

"Actually, I consider myself a *realist*," Ursula said.

"*Anyway*," I said. "If the gentle announcement doesn't work, then we'll investigate, okay?"

"We'll see," was all Miss Pryor would say.

CHAPTER 2
A GENTLE ANNOUNCEMENT

Of course, Anika was absolutely *furious* when we told her about the missing Kangarate the next morning. Julian, Ursula, and I made a special trip to her homeroom to break the news.

"IT WAS STOLEN?!" she burst out.

"Right off her desk," Julian said.

"That's *awful*," Anika said.

"I know," Ursula agreed. "This school is full of crooks."

"You *said* it," Anika said. "We've *got* to get to the bottom of this one."

"But first we have to wait for Miss Pryor to make a 'gentle announcement' during all of her classes to see if Kangarate comes back."

Blitz is early!

"Like *that's* gonna happen," Anika said. "I'll start asking around a bit and see what I can dig up."

Just then, Blitz stumbled in, looking kind of dazed.

"You're *here*!" Anika said. "Early!"

"Yeah," Blitz said. "I have to be on time from now on, or they could hold me back a whole year."

"Yikes," Julian said. "Talk about playing hard ball."

"No kidding," Blitz said.

"How'd you manage to get here?" Anika asked.

"I invented a new alarm system to help me wake up," Blitz explained. "I call it the Snooze Stopper."

"What's it do?" Julian asked.

"Well, it involves lights, music, and mini-golf," Blitz said. "I guess you have to see it to believe it."

Leave it to Blitz to invent a system like that.

"Guess what, Blitz," Anika said. "Miss Pryor's Kangarate got stolen yesterday!"

"NO WAY!"

And so Blitz joined the rest of us in our outrage.

✳ ✳ ✳ ✳

As planned, Miss Pryor made her gentle announcement at the start of our math class that afternoon.

"Yesterday I lost something very special to me," she said. "The last time I saw it, it was right here."

She pointed to the empty spot on her desk.

"If anyone borrowed it, I'd be very happy if you could return it. No questions asked. Just leave it outside my door on Monday morning before school."

"What is it?" someone blurted out.

"It was a birthday present," Miss Pryor said.

And of course, *that* set off a whole explosion of questions...

"Okay, okay, enough," Miss Pryor said. "Yes, it was my birthday yesterday. And the present was a kangaroo toy."

"Yes," Miss Pryor said, looking kind of stunned.

And of course, that set off *another* tidal wave of questions:

"Quiet, please!" Miss Pryor said. "Yes, it was a Kangarate toy. I'm not familiar with the character, but of course I thought it was a very lovely gift."

"Who gave it to you?" someone called out.

I winced, because the last thing I needed was to be called a teacher's pet. But thankfully Miss Pryor didn't give us away.

"That's not important," she said. "What's important is that my gift finds its way back here. I really hope it's waiting for me on Monday morning. Now, please open your books to page..."

And with that, Miss Pryor went on with class. Julian turned to me a little while later.

"I'd say it's about a one-in-a-million chance that Kangarate shows up on Monday morning," he said.

"Who knows," I said. "Maybe it'll break free and hop back here on its own."

"Yeah, *right*," Julian said.

CHAPTER 3
KANGARATE RETURNS?

onday before school we all went to see Miss Pryor.

"Did Kangarate come back?" Ursula asked as soon as we stepped in the door.

"Not yet," Miss Pryor sighed. "But please keep the door closed. I promised I wouldn't look to see who was returning it."

"Do you really, *honestly* think the thief is gonna bring it back?" Ursula asked.

"Yeah," Anika said. "I've never heard of a thief who returns stuff."

"Usually they just take the thing and run for their lives," Julian added.

"Well," Miss Pryor said. "If the thief was a young person, as I think it must have been, then maybe stealing is new to them. Maybe they regret doing it and want a chance to do the right thing."

"*Unlikely*," Ursula said.

"Yeah," Julian agreed. "They'll just want to go have fun with their new Kangarate."

"They'll just be glad they got away with it," Blitz added.

"Well," Miss Pryor sighed. "We'll see."

"Do you think you know who did it?" I asked.

"Oh, no," Miss Pryor said. "I didn't see it happen, so it wouldn't be fair to suspect."

"Did you see anyone near your desk that day?" Ursula asked.

"People go near my desk *every* day," Miss Pryor said. "It's right next to the trash can, remember."

"Has anything ever gone missing from your desk *before*?" Julian asked.

"*No*," Miss Pryor said firmly. "Now, are we done with the interrogation?"

"Sorry," Anika said. "We just *really* want to know who made off with our gift."

"Yeah," Ursula said. "We're starting our investigation today, assuming Kangarate is still missing in action."

"I'm really not comfortable with an investigation," Miss Pryor said. "This is a very delicate matter, and someone could get very upset if they feel they're being falsely accused."

"But Miss *Pryor*," Ursula started to protest, but then we all looked up, because some kids from Miss Pryor's homeroom came in just then.

"Did anyone return the Kangarate?" one of the kids asked as she closed the door behind her.

"I guess that means it's not sitting outside," Anika said.

"Well, let's check," Miss Pryor said, standing up from her desk.

We all followed Miss Pryor over to the door. She opened it up, and we all peeked outside...

But there was no Kangarate anywhere. Miss Pryor looked
really sad.

The halls were starting to fill with kids, and the school day was about to start. It looked like the Kangarate thief was NOT having second thoughts after all.

But then I spotted something.

"WAIT!" I said, pointing at a brown paper bag sitting on the windowsill across the hall.

Miss Pryor brightened up. She went over to the windowsill and grabbed the bag.

"Something's inside," she said, reaching in hopefully.

What's in the bag?

But then we all saw what it was:

Half a buttered bagel.

And an empty bottle of strawberry milk.

"Oh, well," Miss Pryor said. "Too bad."

And so the investigation began.

Someone's leftover breakfast! YUCK!

* * * *

That day at lunch, we met to talk about our game plan.

"I think we'll crack this one pretty fast," Anika said confidently.

"But how?" Julian asked. "We have *nothing* to go on."

"Well, we can make a list of kids in Miss Pryor's classes, especially the ones who sit near Miss Pryor's desk," Anika said. "Then we can talk to those kids and find out if they saw anything."

"Don't you think any witnesses would've come forward by now?" I asked. "There's been a *lot* of buzz about the Kangarate-napping."

"Maybe not," Anika said. "People might be afraid to blow the whistle—especially if the thief's some kind of scary character."

Somehow it seemed a little weird that a "scary character" would want a kangaroo toy, but I guess stranger things have happened.

So anyway, we planned to make our "possible witness" list and start talking to people the next day.

CHAPTER 4
NO PROOF

But the next day at lunch, something happened that changed everything. Anika was the first to hear about it. She ran over to tell me and Julian.

"Guys," she said, totally out of breath. "Ronald has a Kangarate! Over there!"

She pointed in Ronald's direction, and sure enough, he was showing a Kangarate to his friends.

"He's in our math class!" Julian said to me. "He could've taken it *then*!"

We quickly found Ursula and Blitz and filled them in.

"Let's find out what he has to say for himself," Ursula said.

And so we all marched over to confront Ronald.

"Where'd you get *that*?" Ursula asked him.

"At the store," Ronald said. "Where *else* would I get it?"

"Maybe Miss Pryor's desk?" Blitz suggested.

"I *didn't* steal it," Ronald said. "And don't try to say I did."

"Why do you have it at school, then?" Julian asked.

"Everybody was talking about it yesterday," Ronald said. "So I brought mine in to show people. And if *you're* trying to say I took it..."

Ronald got right up in Julian's face. *Whoa.*

"Don't get in my face," Julian warned.

"Don't say I stole stuff!" Ronald shot back.

"Okay, okay," Anika said. "Don't get all *excited*. We're just *asking*."

We all pulled Julian away from Ronald.

"I've had this Kangarate for a LONG time," Ronald said. "Since when you guys were in DIAPERS."

"The cartoon's only been on for *two* years," Blitz argued.

"Like I said," Ronald shot back.

"What*ever*, Ronald," Anika groaned.

"And you know what *else* I have?" Ronald added, reaching into his bag. "You *know* I didn't take *this* from Miss Pryor's desk."

He pulled out Electric Eli, Kangarate's arch enemy.

HA HA HA HA !

Eli, the electric eel

actually gives you a shock when you touch it!

"HA!" Ronald taunted. "Now stand back unless you wanna get shocked."

We all took a step back. Electric Eli could deliver a mean zap if you touched it.

"Whatsamatter?" Ronald taunted. "Ya scared?"

"*Please*," Anika said, rolling her eyes. "We're not scared of a fake eel."

"Yeah," Julian said. "Go play with your toys."

We all walked away as Ronald called after us.

HA HA HA HA LOOOOOOSERS!

obnoxious Ronald

"SCARED YA! HA!"

"That kid is so *whack*," Julian muttered.

Okay, so Ronald was definitely whack, no doubt about it, but it seemed to me like he really *did* collect Kangarate stuff like he said. But not everyone was convinced. In fact, I don't think *anyone* was convinced.

"I bet Ronald only had Electric Eli, and he needed Kangarate to go with it," Blitz said. "So he took Miss Pryor's."

"He's *always* up near her desk trying to steal chalk so he can stick it up his nose," Julian added. "I bet he just grabbed Kangarate while he was at it."

"Maybe if he had the chance to steal *another* Kangarate character, he'd go for it," Blitz suggested. "Maybe we could arrange that."

"You mean we could set a trap?" I asked.

"Exactly," Blitz said. "With *Ninjaroo*. We can put it on Miss Pryor's desk and see if Ronald goes for it."

"Or if anyone *else* goes for it," I added, "in case Ronald's not the one."

"But how are we gonna get our hands on a Ninjaroo?" Anika asked. "They're like sixteen dollars."

Blitz smiled.

"I have one," he said, and then quickly added, "I used to collect Kangarate stuff back in fifth grade."

"Excellent," Anika said.

"But what if Ronald takes it and then denies it?" Ursula asked. "He could just say it was *his* again."

the Ninjaroo trap

"We'll *watch* the trap so we can catch him in the act," Blitz said. "And just in case, I'll write my name on Ninjaroo's shirt tag."

But Ursula wasn't done with her "what-ifs."

"What if Ronald sees the writing and cuts off the tag or something?" Ursula asked.

"Oh, he won't see the writing," Blitz said confidently. "Because I'll use *invisible ink*."

Everyone looked at Blitz with wide eyes.

"You have *invisible ink*?" Anika asked.

"Yup," Blitz said. "I mark a lot of my stuff with it so I can prove it's mine. Video games especially."

"How do *you* see the writing?" Ursula asked.

"I shine a special light on it," Blitz says. "And it shows up."

"Ultraviolet light?" I asked, because I'd heard of that before—I'd just never seen it.

"Exactly," Blitz said.

"What's that?" Julian asked.

"It's this bright purple light that makes the ink glow," Blitz explained. "It's a different *wavelength* from normal light."

"That sounds cool-ee-o, Blitz," Anika said. "Can you bring it tomorrow and show us?"

"Sure," Blitz said. "Or if you guys want to stop by my place after school, I can show you today. *And* I can show you the Snooze Stopper."

"Ooh, we're there," Julian said. "Right, Spencer?"

"Definitely," I said.

As usual, Anika couldn't make it, and Ursula had one of her soccer practices. So Julian and I planned to skip Homework Club and head over to Blitz's place right after school.

CHAPTER 5
BLITZ'S LATEST

At Blitz's place, the first thing Julian and I wanted to see was the Snooze Stopper. So he set it up to show us.

"See, my problem was the snooze button," Blitz explained. "I'd press it and press it and press it and never get out of bed."

"Didn't your parents wake you up?" I asked.

"They tried," Blitz said. "It was really annoying. They'd be yelling and threatening and taking my sheets and all that obnoxious stuff. It's much better to have my own snooze-proof system and cut them out of the picture completely."

before the
Snooze Stopper

BZZZZZZZZZ

snooze button

6:45

GET UP!!!

Then Blitz set off the alarm. Music started blaring out and a bunch of lights in the corner turned on.

"To turn the alarm off," Blitz explained, "I have to stand on those two pads and putt the ball into this hole."

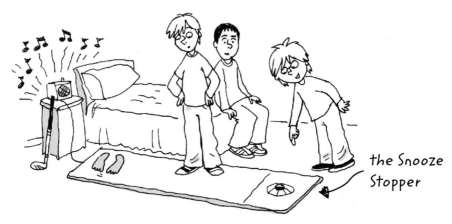

the Snooze Stopper

"Couldn't you just walk over and drop the ball in?" Julian asked.

"No," Blitz said. "My feet have to be on the pads when the ball falls in or the system won't deactivate."

Blitz putted the ball to demonstrate, but he missed by a lot.

"What if you keep missing?" I asked.

"Then I get more and more awake," Blitz said, grabbing the ball and placing it back on the tee. "It's perfect."

"And what if you just ignore the alarm and keep sleeping?" Julian asked.

"The music'll eventually start skipping, and the lights'll start flashing," Blitz said.

"Man, that's *evil*," Julian said with a wince.

"Couldn't you just unplug the alarm?" I asked as Blitz missed his putt *again*.

"It runs on batteries," Blitz said, picking up the alarm case and showing it to us. "I made sure I couldn't get at them easily. And if I tried, I'd be completely awake by the time I unscrewed everything."

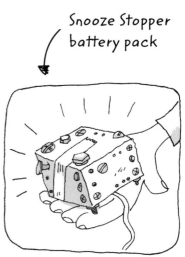

Snooze Stopper battery pack

"Wow," I said. "You really thought this thing out."

"There's a lot at stake," Blitz said. "Another *year* at that school? No, thanks."

Julian and I shuddered.

"Exactly," Blitz said, taking aim with his putter again. This time, finally, the ball dropped into the hole with a clunk, stopping the music mid-note.

"Cool," Julian said.

"It's worked for the past three days," Blitz said, grabbing the ball out of the hole. "I just hope I don't outsmart myself."

Blitz returned the putter to its spot beside his bed.

"Anyway," he continued. "You want to see the invisible ink?"

"Yeah!" Julian and I said.

Blitz went over to his workbench and pulled out a simple metal pen.

"It *looks* like a normal pen," Blitz said, scribbling a note on a piece of scrap paper.

"Like a pen that's out of ink," Julian said.

"Right," Blitz said. "But watch this."

Then Blitz flipped the pen over and shined a purple light on the paper.

"Cool!" Julian said. "Lemme try!"

So Julian and I tried out the pen a couple of times.

"Easy, guys," Blitz said. "We have to save the ink. I only have one of these babies."

Blitz's invisible ink pen

"Where'd you get it?" I asked.

"My mom got it for me at some store downtown," Blitz said. "But the store's out of business now."

"Aw, maaaaan," Julian complained. "The good stores always close."

"But I'm always on the lookout for more," Blitz said, opening his closet door. "I'll hook you guys up if I find any."

Then Blitz started digging through his closet, tossing stuff out as he went.

"Whatcha looking for?" Julian asked.

"Ninjaroo," Blitz answered. "I stuck it in here a couple months ago."

Out flew all kinds of old toys, one after the other, most of them broken or missing body parts, till finally Blitz pulled out a dust-bunny-covered Ninjaroo.

"Here it is," he said with a sneeze.

"That looks *nasty*," Julian said.

"It just needs a little de-dustifying," Blitz said, peeling a giant dust bunny off Ninjaroo's left ear and dropping it on the floor. "And then it'll be good as new. Aren't you guys gonna help?"

So Julian and I helped clean off Ninjaroo. I can't say he really looked good as new when we were done. And he definitely didn't *smell* good as new. But oh well.

dusty Ninjaroo

"Hey, kangaroo stealers can't be choosers," Blitz said.

Then Blitz wrote his name on the tag in the back of Ninjaroo's shirt, and we shined the UV light on it to check.

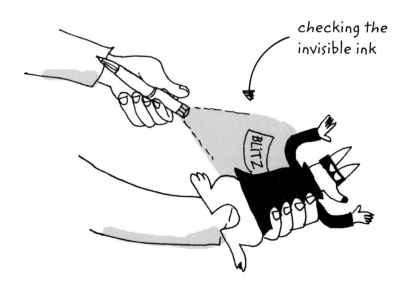

checking the invisible ink

"Ninjaroo is ready for action!" Blitz announced.

"Hope Miss Pryor doesn't have allergies," I said.

"I'll go over him a couple times with the vacuum," Blitz said. "That'll fix him."

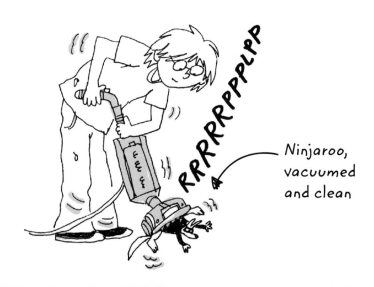

RRRRRPPPLPP

Ninjaroo, vacuumed and clean

The next morning, we all went straight to Miss Pryor's room to fill her in on the plan.

"This is Ninjaroo, Kangarate's sidekick," Blitz said. "See, he kicks to the side. Get it?"

"Very clever," Miss Pryor smiled.

"Can we leave it on your desk to see if someone takes it?" Ursula asked. "We'll take turns keeping watch."

presenting Ninjaroo

Miss Pryor's face suddenly went from smiley to very serious.

"Are you suggesting I set a *trap* on my desk?" she asked.

"Exactly," Ursula said, and we all nodded along with her.

"I'm sorry," Miss Pryor said. "But my desk will *not* be used for a sting operation."

We all looked at Miss Pryor in shock. None of us had imagined for a second that she'd say no.

"BUT MISS PRYOR!" Ursula protested. "How *else* can we find out who stole Kangarate?"

"That matter is over," Miss Pryor said. "I'm very sorry your gift was lost, but there's nothing more we can do about it."

"But we *can*!" Blitz argued. "We can set the trap with Ninjaroo!"

"As the owner of the stolen kangaroo, I say we accept the loss and move on," Miss Pryor said.

"Don't the *givers* of the kangaroo have any rights?" Ursula asked.

"It's not about rights," Miss Pryor said. "It's about taking the most appropriate course of action. In this case, the appropriate thing to do is to learn not to leave tempting new toys on my desk."

"But that's not *satisfying*!" Anika complained.

"Yeah, don't you want *justice*?" Ursula asked.

"Don't you want to know who thinks they can steal stuff off your desk?" Julian asked.

"And don't you want your Kangarate back?" Blitz asked.

"I'm sorry," Miss Pryor said. "But as far as I'm concerned, this case is closed."

✳ ✳ ✳ ✳

Everyone was steaming mad at Miss Pryor after she ruined the plan. We met after lunch to complain about it, and to see if there was anything else we could do to save the investigation. There weren't many ideas.

Anika's list of possible witnesses

Anika had made up her list of possible witnesses, but it was *so* long (three notebook pages), we didn't even know where to start.

"I can't *believe* Miss Pryor wasn't down with the sting," Julian complained for the fiftieth time. "It was so *perfect*."

Then I thought of something.

"Maybe we could still do the sting on our own," I suggested.

"*How?*" everyone asked at once.

"We could scout out other places around school where we could leave Ninjaroo sitting for a while," I said. "Like bookshelves and windowsills."

"Yeah!" Blitz brightened up. "And we can pick places where we *know* Ronald'll be!"

"But what's to stop *anybody* from just helping themselves?" Ursula said. "How are we going to know it's the same person who took Miss Pryor's Kangarate?"

"Yeah," Julian said. "It's gotta be the original crime scene or it's not gonna work right."

"Not necessarily," Anika said. "Most people wouldn't just grab someone else's stuff. And a lot of people wouldn't even *want* a kangaroo toy. It'll be good to see who *does* want it, whether it's Ronald or somebody else."

"I guess it's worth a try," Ursula shrugged.

So we each picked a place where we could put Ninjaroo and keep an eye on it.

"I'll put Ninjaroo next to the dead plants in Mrs. Manning's window during third period," Blitz said. "Ronald's in my class, and he always stares out the window."

"*I'll* put Ninjaroo on Mr. Wyman's trophy shelf," Julian said. "It's near the door, so people'll see it on their way in and out. And Ronald takes *lots* of bathroom breaks."

"I'll try the coat rack in homeroom right before we go down to lunch," Anika said. "Ronald's in my homeroom, and he's always hanging out at the coat rack bothering people."

"I'm going for the microscope shelf in Mr. Lipsky's room," Ursula said. "It's right next to the pencil sharpener, and Ronald likes to grind up markers in there."

"I'll try the bookshelf in the back of my silent reading room," I said. "The trash can's right there."

"But Ronald's not *in* your silent reading class," Blitz said. "He's in mine."

"I know," I said. "But I think we've got Ronald covered. We need to branch out a little."

"Spencer's right," Anika said. "Ronald'll have plenty of chances to snatch Ninjaroo."

"I guess so," Blitz shrugged.

After that, we quickly worked out a schedule for handing off Ninjaroo between classes.

"Cool," Anika said. "Sounds like a plan."

"It's kind of like going fishing," Blitz said.

"For a *rotten* fish," Ursula added.

I think we all thought we'd be the one to make the catch....

CHAPTER 7

CAUGHT IN THE TRAP

But the next day came and went, and no one snatched Ninjaroo. We passed the thing around all day long so it could sit in each of our spots, but either no one noticed or no one cared.

As for Ronald, he was too busy doing his usual stupid stuff to pay any attention.

Ronald

We were all pretty disappointed.

"Maybe we should pick new spots," Julian suggested.

"But how many good spots *are* there in this school?" Anika asked.

Not many.

"Maybe we just have to be patient," Blitz said. "When you go fishing, you spend a lot of time waiting."

"You've been fishing?" Ursula asked.

"No," Blitz said. "I just saw part of a fishing show on TV the other day, and it was really boring like that."

So we decided to stick with our spots for one more day.

The next day during silent reading, I put Ninjaroo in his spot on the cruddy bookshelf in the back. And waited. And waited.

the trap

passing notes

Marisol actually reading

me

talking as usual

As usual, it was pretty crazy during silent reading, so there was plenty of opportunity for the thief to strike, but nothing happened for the whole looooong class.

BUT THEN, at the end of class, to my complete and utter shock—

Someone took Ninjaroo!

And it *wasn't* Ronald sneaking in from the hall or anything like that.

It was someone I would have NEVER EVER EVER EVER EVER EVER EVER EVER EVER EVER EVER EVER EVER expected. Never in a zillion years.

IT WAS MARISOL!

Marisol, the only person who *always* reads during silent reading, every single day.

Marisol with her enormous books.

Marisol who hardly ever speaks.

Marisol who lives in her own world.

CHOMP SLURP MUNCH CRUNCH BURP

It was such a shocker, I didn't know *what* to do. Chase her down the hall and make her hand over the stolen Ninjaroo? Then accuse her of having stolen Kangarate, too?

That was the plan, but I just couldn't do it. No way. I'd never even *spoken* to the girl, and I just couldn't bring myself to get tough with her like that. And I definitely didn't want anyone *else* to get tough with her.

I *had* to come up with some other way to get her to return Ninjaroo (*and* Kangarate, if she'd taken that too). I just needed more time.

angry Ursula

I was standing there totally frozen when Ursula came bursting in. It was her turn to set the trap, so she was expecting me to make a quick handoff.

"Where's Ninjaroo?" she asked quickly.

"Um..." I stalled. "Someone took it."

"WHO?" Ursula demanded, really loud.

And that's when I decided to lie. It was a really quick decision, but something told me it was the right thing to do.

"I don't know," I said with a wince. "I didn't see it happen."

"YOU WEREN'T WATCHING?" she asked, her eyes enormous.

"I *was*," I said. "I just missed it somehow."

"I can't believe it!" Ursula said. "You let Ninjaroo get swiped right from under your nose! What kind of spy are *you*?"

"I'm sorry," I said.

I didn't know what else to say.

"Wait till Blitz hears about *this*," Ursula said. "It was *his* Ninjaroo."

"I know," I said. "I feel terrible."

For the whole rest of the day, I kept going back and forth in my mind about whether or not I'd done the right thing. I couldn't believe I was lying to my friends, and all for this girl I didn't even know.

But I guess it was too late to be thinking all that, since I'd already gone and done it.

✳ ✳ ✳ ✳

Of course, Blitz was *not* happy when he heard the news. Neither was anyone else.

"I'm really sorry," I said. "I'll try to get Ninjaroo back."

"Good luck," Julian said.

"At least it's marked with invisible ink," Anika said. "So if we spot someone with it, we can prove it's ours."

disappointed
Spy Five

"We'll need even *more* good luck for *that* to happen," Ursula said. "Someone dumb like *Ronald* would show off a stolen kangaroo, but this time we *know* it wasn't Ronald."

Everyone looked really depressed.

"Well, at least we have it narrowed down to someone in Spencer's silent reading class," Anika offered again.

"But we *still* can't be sure it's the same person who took Kangarate," Blitz said.

Everyone looked even *more* depressed. I wished I could just tell them it was Marisol, but I kept imagining this:

And I felt like I had to protect her. It was *my* trap she fell into, after all.

"This investigation is a complete mess," Ursula grumbled, slinging her backpack over her shoulder. "Two kangaroos are gone and we're still on square one. I'm going to my clarinet lesson."

"Yeah, I'm outta here, too," Anika said as Ursula marched out the door. "Don't be too depressed, guys."

But of course, it was hard not to be, with Blitz and Julian looking mostly at the floor instead of at me.

CHAPTER 8
SLEEPLESS IN TIMES SQUARE

Things were going pretty rough for me at that point, sorry to say. But fortunately I had two good reasons to put all that bad stuff out of my mind:

1) It was Friday.

2) My dad was showing up on Saturday to visit for a week!

SOUTH POLE
DAD

My dad had decided to come visit so he could see me before he left for his trip to Antarctica (to use some big telescope they have down there). It was kind of a last-minute plan, which is the way Dad usually operates.

When Dad comes to New York (he's been here twice since I moved after my parents got divorced), I go stay with him at his hotel down in Times Square. It's about ten minutes away by cab, but Mom acts like I'm going to Mongolia.

On Saturday afternoon when I was packing my bag, Mom kept trying to get me to take all this useless stuff, as always.

HERE, TAKE THESE GRANOLA BARS.

I'M NOT GOING CAMPING, MOM.

GRANOLA

HOW MUCH UNDERWEAR ARE YOU TAKING? I DON'T THINK YOU TOOK ENOUGH LAST TIME.

WILL YOU STOP?

Fortunately the buzzer rang before Mom could bug me about dental floss and slippers and her other favorite things.

Dad came upstairs to get me and say hi to Mom. They're not on bad terms or anything, at least not in front of me. But it sure is awkward when the two of them try to talk.

* * * *

That night at the hotel, Dad stayed up late working on his laptop as usual. Mom says he's nocturnal (like a bat).

I couldn't sleep because I was thinking a lot about Marisol stealing Ninjaroo (and Kangarate, too, I figured). I kept thinking about what would happen to her if everyone found out.

And *then* I started thinking about the Spy Five being disappointed in me.

With all that on my mind, I ended up getting up and looking out the window at Times Square for a while. It was 2 a.m. and Dad was still typing.

Nothing was okay, of course, but I don't usually talk about stuff like that with my dad.

"Dad," I said, but he didn't hear me, so I said it again louder. "DAD!"

"Yes?"

"Is it okay if I turn on the TV?"

"Sure, but keep the volume down low."

So that's what I did.

$$* \quad * \quad * \quad *$$

On Sunday, Dad and I slept late and then went to some movie about aliens. Dad kept whispering about how they were breaking the laws of physics.

Then Dad went out to get some popcorn and didn't come back for a really long time. Guess he didn't really care if the aliens conquered the universe or not.

Sunday night, Dad worked again, so I had plenty of time to dread going back to school. I tried watching TV to avoid thinking about everything, but then around midnight Dad realized it was a "school night" and made me turn it off.

I wasn't tired at all, so I just lay there thinking about Marisol and her kangaroo problem. For a long time.

angry mob

Run, Marisol!

✳ ✳ ✳ ✳

Of course, the next morning I could *not* wake up for school. I actually slept through homeroom and part of first period. Finally Dad dragged me out of bed and rode with me in the taxi.

That whole day, my eye sockets felt like they were packed full of lead. I kept falling asleep and then waking up all of a sudden when my head came swooping down. Over and over again. It was like torture.

Anika was the first Spy Five person I saw that day.

"Hey, Spencer," she called, catching up with me in the hall. "Whoa, you look REALLY tired."

"I couldn't sleep last night," I said.

"Why?" she asked. "I hope it's not 'cause of what happened Friday with Ninjaroo."

"No," I said, not wanting to admit anything. "It's mainly 'cause I'm staying with my dad, and we were up really late last night."

"Well, don't feel bad about the Ninjaroo thing," Anika said. "'Cause you know what? We're hot on the trail of the kangaroo-napper. I made a list of people in your silent reading class who also have Miss Pryor for math or homeroom, and there's only nine people on it. And *you're* one of them, so that narrows it down to *eight* suspects!"

Anika's suspect list

Angel
Spencer
Jalisa
Natalie
Devon
Cristina
Marisol
Jordan
Leila

I saw Marisol's name on the list, and I thought, *oh no*. But that's all I had the energy to think.

✳ ✳ ✳ ✳

A little later, I ran into Ursula in the hall. I thought she might still be ticked off at me, but she was pretty much back to her usual self.

"Hi Spencer," she said. "You look like you got hit by a truck."

"Thanks," I said.

"Look at my posters," she said proudly. "I made them on my computer over the weekend."

Ursula's posters

"I'm gonna print ten of each," Ursula said. "And then we'll hang them all over school tomorrow during first period. Want to help?"

"Are we *allowed* to hang posters like that?" I asked.

"We're just gonna hang them," Ursula shrugged. "The teachers can take them down if they don't like them. As long as they're up for a little while, they'll do their job. Here, take one of each."

She handed me one of each poster and dashed off down the hall, leaving me to stumble to my next class.

✳ ✳ ✳ ✳

Next I saw Julian and Blitz.

"Spencer!" Julian called. "Where *were* you this morning?"

"I overslept," I said.

"You need the Snooze Stopper!" Blitz said. "Really, I can build you one!"

"I just need to get to sleep before three in the morning," I said.

"*Man*," Julian said. "No wonder you look like that."

"Have you heard the rumor we started?" Blitz asked.

"What rumor?" I asked.

"We started a rumor that the thief was actually spotted in the act," Julian said. "And the teachers are giving the thief till Friday to return the kangaroos before they call the cops."

"Spread the word," Blitz said.

Yikes, I thought. Things were really getting out of hand.

And what was I supposed to do about it? Unfortunately my foggy brain had no ideas to offer up.

And then I thought maybe there was someone who could help....

Miss Pryor was marking papers at her desk when I stopped by.

"Spencer," she said. "I saw you nodding off during class today. You *really* look exhausted."

"I was up till three," I explained.

"MY GOODNESS!" she gasped. "I certainly hope you're not planning to make a habit of that."

"No," I said. "I just couldn't sleep last night."

"Why not?" she asked.

I took a deep breath.

"Miss Pryor," I began. "I think I know who took your Kangarate. If I tell you, it'll just be between you and me, and the person won't get in trouble, right?"

Miss Pryor put down her marking pen and looked at me very seriously.

confessing to Miss Pryor

"Of course," she said quietly.

"It was Marisol," I said.

Miss Pryor looked down at her papers and sighed.

"What makes you think that?" she asked.

"Because I saw her steal Ninjaroo," I said.

"That other kangaroo?" she asked. "You set your trap after all?"

"In another class," I nodded, wincing because I knew what was next.

"I *told* you not to do that," Miss Pryor said, shaking her head. "Sometimes it's better just to let things go."

"I didn't tell anyone," I said. "I didn't want Marisol to have to face them."

"You're right to protect her," Miss Pryor said. "This whole situation makes me very sad."

"Why do you think she'd *do* something like that?" I asked.

"I don't know," Miss Pryor said, thinking for a second. "I imagine there are a lot of things she wishes she could have. Maybe she has a special fondness for kangaroos. I really can't say. But it's *very* unlike her to do something like this."

"Do you think maybe she took them for a little brother or sister?" I asked, because Marisol just didn't seem like she'd be into kangaroo toys.

"She doesn't have any brothers or sisters," Miss Pryor said. "She lives alone with her father."

"Not her mother?"

"No," Miss Pryor said. "Just her father."

I was going to ask where her mother was, but I could tell Miss Pryor didn't want to say much more about Marisol's personal stuff.

"So what should I *do*?" I asked. "I don't want the others to find out it's her. They're out for *blood*."

"I don't know, Spencer," Miss Pryor said. "It's a tough one. Since you saw her take the other kangaroo, maybe you can think of a nice way to ask for it back."

Talk to Marisol? About *this*? Never.

"I can't," I said. "Can't *you*? She took *your* kangaroo, too."

"We don't know that for certain," Miss Pryor reminded me.

"But can't you help anyway?" I asked.

"I think you'll find a nice way to handle this, Spencer," she said. "Think about it. If you're really stuck, let me know. But I'm sure you'll think of a way."

How could I think of a way, when I was so wiped out my brain was like a pile of mashed potatoes?

All I could really think about was getting back to the hotel so I could sleep.

HOW WAS SCHOOL?

So I thanked Miss Pryor for helping (not very much) and dragged myself out of school and onto the subway.

When I finally got to the hotel, I nose-dived onto the bed as soon as I stepped in the door.

hat night I woke up around ten. I was STARVING, so I ordered pizza from room service and drank a soda from the mini-bar. Dad said he wasn't hungry. I think he just runs on coffee, actually.

I probably *did* have homework, but school was all a blur so I couldn't remember. I figured I'd deal with it some other time.

After I ate, I felt totally awake for the first time all day, so I started thinking more about the Marisol problem. I was almost positive she'd taken both kangaroos—especially since she was on Anika's suspect list.

I wondered *why* she wanted those kangaroos, and if she felt guilty at all for taking them. Maybe she was scared people would find out. Maybe she had to hide them from her father, because if he saw them, he'd figure out what she'd done. I wondered what her father was like. Was he nice to her? Was he busy all the time like mine? Did Marisol miss having her Mom around? I wondered a *lot* of things about Marisol's life in general.

Then I wondered how Marisol would react if she heard Julian and Blitz's rumor, or what she'd do when she saw all of Ursula's posters. Would she:

A) Give in and return the kangaroos, or

B) Hold tight and wait till the whole thing blew over?

I wondered if there was anything I could do to convince her to pick choice A. I knew I couldn't *talk* to her. That would be way too embarrassing for *both* of us.

So I decided I'd write her a note and slip it onto her chair right before silent reading. A note like this:

Please return the Kangaroo(s). You'll be glad you did.

my note to Marisol

And then I started thinking about how I *knew* she'd be glad. I knew for a reason I'd never told anybody in this whole world.

I knew because one time, last year, when I still lived in Maryland, I stole something. And that's when I pulled out my sketch pad and started drawing the story.

The *PERMANENT MARKER*

I WAS IN THE SCHOOL SUPPLY STORE WITH MY MOM WHEN I SAW IT.

Permie

IT WAS A BLACK FINE TIP **PERMANENT MARKER** —PERFECT FOR MY DRAWINGS.

PERMANENT INK IS BETTER 'CAUSE WHEN YOU GO OVER PENCIL WITH REGULAR INK, IT SOMETIMES SMEARS WHEN YOU ERASE THE PENCIL LINES.

OH MAN!

SO I ASKED MY MOM IF I COULD GET IT.

I COULDN'T BELIEVE SHE'D BE SO UNREASONABLE, AND THAT I WAS GOING TO HAVE TO PUT THAT MARKER BACK AND WALK AWAY.

IT WASN'T LIKE I COULD JUST COME BACK LATER AND BUY IT MYSELF, 'CAUSE WHERE I LIVED YOU HAD TO DRIVE TO GET TO STORES. AND MY DAD HAD ALREADY MOVED TO COLORADO AT THAT POINT, SO THERE WAS NO WAY I COULD GET HIM TO TAKE ME.

SO I DECIDED TO DO SOMETHING I'D NEVER DONE BEFORE. I STUFFED THE MARKER INTO MY JACKET POCKET.

I FIGURED IT WASN'T THAT BIG A DEAL, 'CAUSE THE PEN WAS ONLY 89¢. IT WASN'T LIKE I WAS STEALING A BIG THING. THAT'S WHAT I KEPT TELLING MYSELF AS I STOOD NEXT TO MY MOM AT THE CHECKOUT.

THE SCARIEST PART WAS WALKING THROUGH THE DOOR, PAST THE **SECURITY GUY.**

WHEN HE LOOKED AT ME, I FELT LIKE HE KNEW, BUT HE DIDN'T.

THAT NIGHT I USED THE PEN — IT WAS AS GOOD AS I THOUGHT IT WOULD BE.

IT _DID_ SMELL BAD THOUGH.

I HID THE PEN INSIDE AN OLD SHOE IN MY CLOSET, SO MY MOM WOULDN'T FIND IT.

AT SCHOOL THAT WEEK, I KEPT WORRYING THAT MOM WOULD SOMEHOW FIND THE PEN. BUT SHE DIDN'T.

THEN ABOUT A WEEK AFTER I STOLE THE PEN, SOMETHING BAD HAPPENED — IT ROLLED OFF MY DESK...

...AND LANDED ON MY PANTS, LEAVING A **PERMANENT** BLACK MARK!

OF COURSE I WASN'T ABOUT TO LET MOM SEE _THAT_, SO I THOUGHT ABOUT HIDING MY PANTS, OR THROWING THEM OUT ALTOGETHER.

BUT THEN I THOUGHT SHE'D NOTICE THEY WERE MISSING, SO INSTEAD I CUT OUT THE PART WITH THE STAIN.

MOM SAW THE HOLE THE NEXT TIME SHE DID LAUNDRY. SHE GOT MAD, BUT IT BLEW OVER.

HOW'D THIS HAPPEN?

DUNNO

IT DIDN'T STOP THERE, THOUGH. IT GOT _WORSE_. A FEW NIGHTS LATER, I HAD THE PEN SITTING OPEN ON MY DESK, AND I LEANED ON IT...

...AND I GOT A STAIN ON MY **ARM**!

A PERMANENT STAIN ON MY <u>ARM</u>? WOULD IT BE LIKE A TATTOO ON ME FOR **LIFE**? HOW WAS I SUPPOSED TO KEEP <u>THAT</u> HIDDEN?

I TRIED SCRUBBING IT.

BUT THE STAIN WASN'T GOING ANYWHERE. I ACTUALLY FELT KIND OF SICK, TOO. MAYBE THE TOXIC INK WAS SEEPING INTO MY BLOOD. MAYBE I WOULD DIE FROM INK POISONING, OR MAYBE IT WOULD STUNT MY GROWTH.

TOXIC INK BOY

I HATED THAT MARKER. IT WAS LIKE A CURSE.

HA HA

HA

HA

Permie

I PUT THE PEN IN MY JACKET POCKET SO I COULD THROW IT OUT THE NEXT DAY AT SCHOOL.

BUT AS I LAY IN MY BED THAT NIGHT, I THOUGHT ABOUT THAT MARKER, AND I DECIDED I HAD TO SET THINGS STRAIGHT.

HA HA

I HAD TO LIFT THE CURSE.

MOM, CAN WE GO TO THE SCHOOL SUPPLY STORE THIS WEEKEND?

SURE, WHAT DO YOU NEED?

STUFF

SO I WALKED INTO THE STORE WITH THE PEN IN MY POCKET, PAST THE SECURITY GUY AGAIN.

AND I PUT THE MARKER BACK.

I FELT SO MUCH BETTER THAT DAY. MY SLATE WAS CLEAN. NOTHING TO WORRY ABOUT, NOTHING TO HIDE ANYMORE.

EXCEPT MY STAIN...

...BUT EVEN THAT WENT AWAY AFTER A WHILE. IT GOT LIGHTER AND LIGHTER, TILL FINALLY IT WAS GONE.

✻ ✻ ✻

By the time I finished drawing the whole story, it was 3:30 in the morning. I hadn't even noticed the time passing—it was like the clock jumped five hours in a snap.

Good thing Dad didn't give me a hard time about staying up late. I guess he could tell I really had my mind set on getting that story done.

The story wasn't for *me*, you see—it was for Marisol. This might sound crazy, but I thought I'd give it to her instead of the note. I just thought it would be a good thing for her to read it.

"Looks like we're both night owls," Dad said.

"Guess so," I said.

As I folded up the story and stuck it in my backpack, I wondered how Marisol would react when she read it the next day in silent reading. Would she realize it was from me? I didn't put my name on it, but she might have heard that I draw all the time, and maybe she'd recognize me in the pictures.

Or maybe she didn't know the first thing about me and wouldn't recognize me at all.

Either way, I just hoped she'd like the story and do the right thing because of it. Maybe it was a strange thing to do, but hey, I'm Spencer Strange.

night owls

The next morning, of course, I couldn't wake up for school again. Fortunately Dad had no problem writing me another excuse.

> SPENCER HAD AN APPOINTMENT THIS MORNING...
>
> ...WITH DR. SLEEP.

When I got to school, it was the middle of second period, and Ursula's posters were already up.

By lunchtime, even though the teachers had already taken most of the posters down, *everyone* was talking about them, especially my crowd.

"We've definitely got the thief running scared now," Ursula said. "*Ha.*"

I saw Marisol at one of the tables, with her nose buried in a book. Every so often, she would look up and stare out into space. I wondered what was going through her mind.

"Spencer, snap out of it," Anika said. "You're like a zombie."

"And you look like you got socked in both eyes," Ursula added.

"Sure you don't want a Snooze Stopper?" Blitz asked. "I'm working on Version 1.2, the basketball model."

"I'll be okay," I said. "I'm gonna catch up on my sleep tonight."

✳ ✳ ✳ ✳

That day I got to my silent reading class early and left the story on Marisol's chair. It took a while for Marisol to show up, so the room was already full of kids by the time she walked in.

I watched out of the corner of my eye as Marisol went over to her desk and pulled out her chair.

But as I was watching, groups of kids kept walking by and blocking my view, so I couldn't tell if she'd seen the story or not. As far as I could see, she just sat down, opened up her book, and started to read, like any day.

I kept watching her the whole class, looking for any sign that she was reading my story. I wondered if maybe she had it behind her book or something. But I couldn't say for sure.

Then, at the end of class, Marisol closed her book, got up, pushed in her chair, and walked out of the room. After she was gone, I casually walked over to her side of the room as if I was going to check out something on the bookshelf. When I passed her desk, I glanced at her chair.

The story was still there.

Had she not even noticed it? She *was* the kind of girl who kept her nose in a book, after all. She didn't pay attention to *anything* but her book in silent reading.

I quickly grabbed the story and made my way out of the room. I unfolded it carefully, looking for any sign that it had been unfolded and refolded. I couldn't find any.

So I went back to the hotel that day completely depressed.

✳ ✳ ✳ ✳

I *thought* I was going to get some sleep that night, but as it turned out, Dad's friend invited us to look at Saturn through a telescope on the roof of some building. I could actually see the rings. Dad was all excited.

By the time we got back to the hotel, I was just about dead.

CAN YOU SEE 'EM?

YEAH!

✱ ✱ ✱ ✱

The next morning, I decided I was absolutely *not* going to school.

"I think this counts as me being officially sick," I said. "I feel like I fell off a building."

Dad agreed, so I slept till eleven.

"We're going to have to be better about school next time," Dad said.

But I could tell he was just saying that because he knew he was supposed to.

Anyway, that day Dad said he wanted to take me to a modern art museum, because of me being an artist. So we went. It was VERY weird.

Then, as we were leaving, Dad started asking me personal questions.

"Is everything okay? You seem upset," he said.

"I'm okay," I lied, figuring he'd give up.

But he didn't.

"Is it your school?" Dad asked. "Because if you're not happy there, there are lots of good schools in this city you could try instead. My colleague was telling me about a school where the kids go to a *museum* every week..."

"It's not *that*," I said.

"Then what is it?" he asked.

"Dad, can we go to a toy store?" I suddenly blurted out.

"Why?" he asked.

"I'll tell you when we get there," I bargained.

When we got to the toy store, I took Dad right to the aisle with the Kangarate toys.

"Will you buy me these?" I asked, pointing to Kangarate and Ninjaroo.

"You want kangaroo toys? Aren't you a little old for those?" he asked.

"No—they're for *all* ages," I said. "Will you get them for me? Please?"

"I just don't understand why you want them so much," Dad said. "Does this have something do with why you're upset?"

And so I had no choice but to tell him the whole story of Marisol and the kangaroos, right there in the toy store.

"So will you get them for me?" I asked when I finished.

Dad thought for a moment.

"You're telling me that you have a class where you just sit there and *read*?" he asked. "What's the point of that?"

"I don't know, Dad, they just make us do it," I said, trying to get back to the point. "So will you buy me the kangaroos?"

Dad thought for *another* moment.

"So, you think if you give that girl these new kangaroos, she'll return the other two?" Dad asked. He seemed kind of skeptical.

"She'll have no reason to keep them," I nodded.

"I don't know, Spencer," Dad said. "But if you feel strongly that this is the right thing to do, I'll certainly help you."

"THANKS!" I said, grabbing Kangarate and Ninjaroo from the shelves.

"I *knew* you weren't really interested in kangaroo toys," Dad said. "You usually just want *spy* gear."

"Actually," I said. "I could use some of that, too."

And I started telling him about Blitz's UV pen, and about how much I wanted one, and about how I'd even looked online and found a store that sold them.

"Me and my big mouth," Dad said.

CHAPTER 11
THE RIGHT THING TO DO

The next morning I had the hotel's front desk give me a wake-up call. I got out of bed, got dressed, stuffed Kangarate and Ninjaroo into my backpack, hopped on the subway, and made it to school early!

The plan was to give the kangaroos to Marisol during silent reading. I had come up with a good way to give them to her, and it involved my silent reading teacher, so I wanted to talk with her about it before school. I hoped she'd go along with the idea (I'll explain the whole thing later).

But before I went to my silent reading classroom, I stopped in to see Julian in homeroom.

"SPENCER!" he said when he saw me. "WHERE'VE YOU BEEN?"

"I had to take a day off," I said. "I was exhausted."

"DID YOU HEAR?!" he asked.

"No," I said. "What?"

"THE KANGAROOS CAME BACK!"

"Whoa!" I said, feeling incredibly happy all of a sudden. "*Both* of them?"

WHERE'VE YOU BEEN?

"Yeah," Julian said. "Miss Pryor found them both outside her room yesterday morning. Come on—let's go see Anika and Blitz."

So we ran down to Anika and Blitz's homeroom. We found Ursula in there with Anika, but no sign of Blitz.

"Spencer, did you *hear*?" Anika asked. "Kangarate and Ninjaroo are back!"

"Yeah, Julian just told me," I said. "But are we *sure* Miss Pryor didn't buy new ones, just to put an end to the whole thing?"

I could imagine Miss Pryor doing that.

"Definitely not," Ursula said. "Blitz checked Ninjaroo's tag with the UV light, and it was the same one, all right."

"Don't doubt it, Spencer," Anika said. "Be happy!"

"My posters must have done the trick!" Ursula said proudly.

"No, no, no," Julian said. "It was the *rumor* that did it."

"You don't even *know* if the thief heard the rumor," Ursula said. "I *know* the thief saw my posters."

"They were up for like five minutes before the teachers took 'em all down," Julian argued.

"They didn't get *all* of them down till third period!" Ursula shot back.

"ANYWAY," I said, trying to prevent an actual brawl. "Do we know who did it?"

"No," Ursula said. "But I have my suspicions."

"Who?" I asked, feeling a little nervous.

"Devin Burton," Ursula said. "That nose-picker from my science class."

"No way," Julian argued. "Devin doesn't care about Kangarate stuff. I bet it was Jordan Johnson..."

And so they went on arguing. I wondered if they'd ever just let it go, or if I'd eventually have to tell them it was Marisol. I was thinking about that when Anika said:

"Hey, where's Blitz?"

"Hmmm," I said, looking at the clock. "Hope the Snooze Stopper didn't conk out."

"That'd be a shame," Anika said. "He's been here early for two weeks straight."

After a few more minutes of listening to Julian and Ursula's raging debate (and no sign of Blitz), we all had to head back to our homerooms.

Even though I *still* wasn't sure what I was going to tell the Spy Five, I felt happier than I had in a long, long time, knowing that Marisol had done the right thing.

✳ ✳ ✳ ✳

That day in math, Miss Pryor made a point of coming over to my desk before class started.

"We missed you yesterday," she said.

"I wasn't feeling too well," I explained.

"I'm glad things are better now," she said with a smile. "I'm sure you know about the surprise that was waiting for me yesterday."

"Yeah," I said.

"Well done," she said with a smile.

"I didn't have anything to do with it," I said.

"Oh, I'm sure you had *a lot* to do with it," she said.

"Really, I didn't," I insisted.

"Give yourself some credit, Spencer. You handled it very well," Miss Pryor said, then smiled and walked away.

* * * *

Finally, at the end of the day, it was time for silent reading class. I got there early, because I still wanted to try to make my kangaroo plan happen. Fortunately Mrs. Kleinman was alone in the room when I got there, so I went up to her desk with Kangarate and Ninjaroo.

"Mrs. Kleinman, my father wanted to give a reward to the person who does the most reading," I said, handing her the kangaroos. "These are for the winner."

Mrs. Kleinman looked stunned.

"Your father wants to give two kangaroos to the person who's read the most books?"

"Yes," I nodded.

"But why kangaroos?" she asked. "Does he know that these very same kangaroos were stolen at school recently?"

"Yeah, he knows," I said with a shrug. "I guess he figured they'd be a good prize 'cause they were so in demand. But you don't have to say they were from *him* or anything. They're just a prize for...whoever's earned it."

"How strange," she said.

"That *is* my dad's name," I said. "And mine."

Mrs. Kleinman laughed.

"Well," she said. "I'm sure you know who wins the kangaroo prize."

Mrs. Kleinman pointed to the chart where she kept track of everyone's reading. For each book we read, we get a star, and Marisol's stars went all the way off the chart.

"It's not even close," I said. "Marisol's just unstoppable."

At that point, most of the class had arrived, so it was getting really loud. I turned to look for Marisol, and there she was, as usual, already reading at her seat.

When the bell rang, Mrs. Kleinman quieted everyone down and, when people were finally settled, she made the announcement.

"I have very exciting news," she said. "Thanks to a generous donation, we have a prize for the person who's read the most books so far this year. And I don't think anyone will be surprised when I say that the winner is..."

"**MARISOL!**" everyone said at once.

"Congratulations, Marisol!" she said. "Here's your prize!"

And *wow*, you should have seen Marisol's face when she saw the kangaroos! It was like she'd won a hundred-million-dollar jackpot.

"Kangarate and Ninjaroo *again!*" someone shouted. "Man, that's all you hear about at this school these days!"

"I guess word must have gotten around that kangaroo toys are popular here," Mrs. Kleinman said.

"Is there gonna be another prize?" someone else asked. "Like next semester?"

"Yeah!" everyone agreed.

"I don't know," Mrs. Kleinman said. "We'll have to see."

And then the chorus started:

"**OH, COME ON!**"   "**PLEASE!**"

"**MAYBE I'LL ACTUALLY READ!**"

"**PLEEEEASE!**"

"Well, I imagine something could be arranged," Mrs. Kleinman said. "If there's so much interest."

"YES!" everyone said at once.

"But we have to start over," someone argued. "'Cause Marisol's so far ahead, no one could ever catch up."

"That sounds fair," Mrs. Kleinman said.

But of course, I was sure it wouldn't take long for Marisol to leave everyone in the dust again.

That day, silent reading class was a complete shocker, because for the first time all year, EVERYONE ACTUALLY READ. It's kind of amazing Mrs. Kleinman never thought of giving out prizes before. You could tell she was realizing that herself.

I couldn't really concentrate on my book that much, because my mind was still spinning with all the crazy things that had happened that week. I looked over at Marisol and her kangaroos, and I just felt glad that she'd done the right thing and still got to have what she wanted.

I *still* wondered *how* she'd decided to return the stolen stuff—was it because of the posters or the rumors or just her own guilty conscience?

And that's when I noticed there was a piece of paper sticking out of my desk.

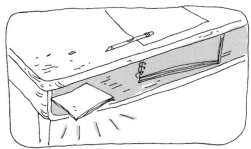

And I unfolded it to see, to my complete surprise:

drawn by Marisol

I could hardly believe it! She must have read the story after all! And she must have realized it was ME who drew it! Had she decided to return the kangaroos because of me?

I looked over to see if she might look back at me, but of course she never looked up from her book. Even when she walked out of class that day, she didn't look at me. Funny— I wondered if she ever would.

✳ ✳ ✳ ✳

After silent reading, I ran into Blitz in the hall.

"What happened this morning?" I asked him. "Did the Snooze Stopper break down?"

"No," Blitz said. "It's working, all right. The problem is that now I can sink that putt in my sleep. I got it on the first try this morning and just went right back to bed. I think I even continued the same dream."

"Oh, sorry," I said. "But look on the bright side—maybe someday you can go pro."

"But first I have to graduate from this school," Blitz said. "So tonight I'm upgrading to Version 2.1—the basketball model."

Blitz as a pro golfer?

"Good luck," I said.

Somehow I couldn't exactly see Blitz in the NBA.

* * * *

That day after school, I met with the Spy Five to give them the *other* thing I'd bought with my dad. Invisible ink pens—one for everyone!

"Where'd you get 'em?" Blitz asked excitedly.

"I found a company online, and they had a store in the city," I explained. "So I went there yesterday with my dad and picked these up. I figured they'd be good for passing around secret messages."

"*And* we can use them to mark our stuff in case it gets stolen," Julian added.

"Thanks, Spencer!" Ursula said, and the others chimed in with their thanks, too.

While they were all trying out their pens, Anika slipped me a note.

"Check it out," she whispered.

So I shined my light on the paper and saw...

Anika's secret

I KNOW IT WAS MARISOL. MEET ME IN THE HALL IN TWO MINUTES.

I felt a rush of horror. How did she know? And how *much* did she know?

"I gotta run to Miss Manning's room for a second, guys," Anika said. "I'll be back in a few."

About two minutes later, I slipped out, too, saying I had to go to the bathroom.

Anika was waiting for me at the end of the hall. She motioned for me to follow her down the stairs.

"How did you *know?*" I asked as we made our way downstairs. "And how come you didn't *tell* me?"

"Never talk in stairwells, Spencer," Anika said. "Your voice echoes, and you never know who's above or below."

"Good point," I said.

When we got downstairs, she told me the whole story.

"Since the posters went up the other day, I thought I'd keep an eye on Miss Pryor's room in the morning in case the kangaroos came back," she explained. "And yesterday morning, I saw Marisol leaving the kangaroos there."

"You *did?*" I asked, totally in shock.

"Yup," Anika said. "And I actually talked with her about it."

"What did you *say?*" I gasped.

Marisol caught in the act

"Oh, mostly I just listened," she said. "She told me how she'd seen all the posters and heard all the rumors, and even found a little comic book on her chair from *somebody.*"

I felt my face turn red.

"I guess she thought no one would really care if she took those two kangaroos," Anika continued. "Since things *do* disappear around this school a lot. But then she became Public Enemy #1."

"No kidding," I said. "That's why I didn't want to tell anybody."

"You could have told *me,*" Anika insisted.

"I know," I said. "I should have. Things just went totally out of control after it happened. I didn't know *who* to tell *what.*"

"So you actually saw Marisol take Ninjaroo?" Anika asked.

"Yeah," I said. "And when Ursula came in, I didn't know what to do, so I lied."

"Hmmm...sounds like *somebody* has a little sweet spot for Marisol," Anika said with a smile.

I felt my face get even REDDER.

"No," I said quickly. "I just didn't want her to get humiliated. She's so nice and quiet and private and all. I was really shocked that it was her."

"So was I," Anika said.

"Did she say why she wanted those kangaroos?" I asked.

"I guess she's a huge fan of Kangarate and Ninjaroo, but her dad won't let her collect the stuff 'cause he says it's for boys," Anika explained. "So she just helped herself when she had the chance."

"Does anyone else know?" I asked.

"Just Miss Pryor," she said. "'Cause she came by while I was talking with Marisol."

I gasped.

Marisol confessing

"Marisol was okay about confessing the whole thing like that?" I asked.

"Oh, she was okay about it, 'cause we promised we'd keep it hush-hush," Anika said. "I think she felt a lot better coming clean like that. And I'm sure she's really *a lot* better now that she's got her own kangaroos."

"Man, you really find out about *everything*," I said, completely amazed.

"Yeah, you can't keep a secret from *me* around this school," Anika said. "But don't worry, I'll make sure this one *stays* secret."

"Even from the rest of the Spy Five?" I asked. "They're still trying to figure out who it was."

"Well, now that the kangaroos are back and they're not raging mad about it anymore, it might be okay," Anika said. "And you know, someone like Ursula's not gonna give up till she finds out who it was."

"I think we should tell them," I said, feeling very sure all of a sudden, now that I had Anika onboard. "I'll just tell them I figured it out using your suspect list. You know, by process of elimination."

"Okay, let's do it," Anika said. "You want to go back first? I'll give you about a minute. But don't tell 'em till I get back. I want to see the looks on their faces! *And* I can back you up on the suspect list."

"Gotcha," I said.

"By the way," Anika said as I turned to go. "That was a really nice thing you did for Marisol, looking out for her like that."

How *embarrassing*.

I didn't know what to say, so I just smiled and took off as fast as possible.

✳ ✳ ✳ ✳

As promised, I waited till Anika got back and then broke the news.

"Guys, there's something I have to tell you." I said. "Do you promise not to freak out?"

"Yeah," they all said cautiously.

"I know who the kangaroo thief was," I said.

"WHO?" they all asked with enormous eyes. Even Anika played along.

"Remember you promised not to freak out," I said. "And it *has* to stay a secret, just between us five."

"Who was it?" Julian asked impatiently.

"*Marisol,*" I whispered.

"THAT BOOKWORM GIRL?" Ursula said really loud.

"Shhh!" everyone said.

"Believe it or not," I said. "It was her."

"How'd you know?" Blitz asked.

"Anika had it narrowed down to just eight suspects," I said. "And I knew a couple of those people were absent the day Ninjaroo went missing. I *also* happen to know Marisol's really into Kangarate."

"REALLY?" Blitz said.

"I heard that, too," Anika said. "She even has a Kangarate key chain, you know."

"*Her?*" Julian asked.

"Yeah," Anika said. "She was *my* prime suspect, too. And then—here's the clincher—I know for a fact she was spotted outside Miss Pryor's room yesterday morning."

"WHOA!" Ursula said. "Why didn't you *say* anything?"

"I wanted to be sure," Anika said.

"Me too," I said, smiling at Anika.

"Now that you mention it," Ursula said. "I *do* remember seeing her looking at one of my posters with her face like this..."

Ursula made her face look horrified.

"But I *never* would have considered her a suspect," Ursula continued. "I guess I was expecting it to be someone obnoxious like Ronald."

"If she wanted Kangarate and Ninjaroo so much, why couldn't she just buy her own?" Blitz asked.

"Was it because of...money or something?" Ursula asked with a wince.

"I think that might've been part of it," Anika said. "That's why we have to keep it under wraps so we don't embarrass her. She *did* do the right thing, after all."

Everyone was kind of quiet.

"She can just *have* my Ninjaroo if she wants it," Blitz offered. "And I even have an old Kangarate, too. It might not have a head, though."

"Oh, she's all set," I said. "My silent reading teacher agreed to give prizes for reading the most books in our class, and the first prize she gave out today was Kangarate and Ninjaroo. Of course you *know* who won."

"Something tells me *you* had something to do with that," Ursula said.

"*Maybe,*" I said with a smile.

"Wow," Julian said. "You had it covered, Spencer."

"I would've filled you guys in sooner," I said. "It's just been a crazy, crazy week."

That was for sure.

✳ ✳ ✳ ✳

That night my dad was heading back to Colorado, so he dropped me off at my apartment after dinner. Of course, Dad was really happy to hear that the kangaroo problem had worked out okay, and that the Spy Five really liked the pens he bought. I guess I'll be seeing him when he gets back from the South Pole in a few weeks. He even said he'd bring me back some actual melted iceberg.

Anyway, Mom was really overjoyed to see me. As usual, it was like I'd been gone for months on a trip to outer space or something. She wanted to hear about *everything*, but of course I just told her the Mom-rated version.

So, anyway, another Spy Five adventure is over, and I have to say, this was the trickiest one yet. At least for me.

6R

It was tough keeping a secret from my friends and then figuring out what to share and what NOT to share in the end. But I guess spies have to be able to do stuff like that.

Until next time,

— Spencer

Happy
Mom

P.S. Ursula found out Miss Pryor's age. She clinched it with the Chinese zodiac question, just like she said she would.

P.P.S. But then we all realized it wasn't that exciting after all.

P.P.P.S. Poor Ursula.

Spy Gear Manual
Invisible Ink Pens with UV Lights

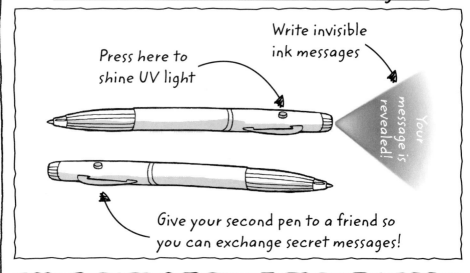

Press here to shine UV light

Write invisible ink messages

Your message is revealed!

Give your second pen to a friend so you can exchange secret messages!

Groovy UV Idea #1:

Write your secret invisible ink messages in the margins of regular visible notes. That way, people'll just think you're passing an innocent note. If you pass a blank paper, people will know something's up!

obvious invisible ink message

Yes, there's an invisible message here!

I think Ronald's on to us.

Hey, let's hang out at my place after school today. I can show you this new video game I got.

Be careful what you say.

undercover invisible ink message

Groovy UV Idea #2:

If you keep a journal, write the secret parts in UV ink. That way, if some snooper ever tries to read your secrets, the important details will be safe.

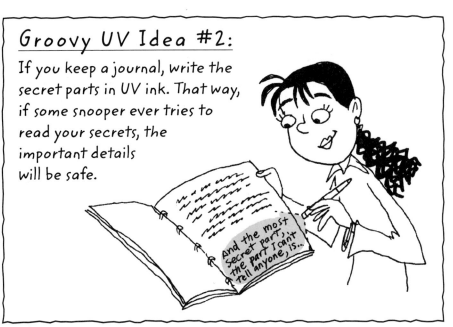

Julian Says:

Mark your important stuff in invisible ink. That way, if it ever gets lost or stolen, you'll be able to prove it's yours.

UV Tip #1:

Don't press too hard when you write, or you'll make grooves in the paper that people will be able to see!

UV Games

People who try to catch spies have to be good at <u>finding</u> invisible ink messages. To test <u>your</u> spy-catching skills, gather a pile of ten papers (magazine pages, old junk mail—you name it) and have a friend write a secret message somewhere on one of them.

How fast can you find the invisible message? Then switch roles, and see if your friend can find your note faster. Who's the #1 spy catcher?

UV Tip #2:

Read your UV messages in a darkened room—they'll glow even brighter!

Have fun keeping your secrets out of sight!

— Spencer